Thanks, Camilla Blua! —R.A.

Text copyright © 2020 by Chiara Carminati
Illustrations copyright © 2020 by Roberta Angaramo
All Rights Reserved
HOLIDAY HOUSE is registered in the U.S. Patent and Trademark Office.
Printed and bound in March 2020 at Toppan Leefung, DongGuan City, China.
The artwork was created with crayons and acrylic paints on Fabriano watercolor paper
www.holidayhouse.com
First Edition
1 3 5 7 9 10 8 6 4 2

Library of Congress Cataloging-in-Publication Data

Names: Carminati, Chiara, author. | Angaramo, Roberta, illustrator.
Title: Smile, Breathe, and Go Slowly: slumby the sloth goes to school
by Chiara Carminati ; illustrated by Roberta Angaramo.
Description: First edition. | New York : Holiday House, [2020]
Audience: Ages 3–7 | Audience: Grades K–1
Summary: Slumby is well-liked at school, but being too slow to play
with his classmates at recess makes him sad until Armadillo gets in trouble
and only Slumby can save him.
Identifiers: LCCN 2019025611 | ISBN 9780823442461 (hardcover)
ISBN 9780823443871 (epub)
Subjects: CYAC: Sloths—Fiction. | Schools—Fiction. | Speed—Fiction.
Classification: LCC PZ7.1.C415 Slo 2020 | DDC [E]—dc23
LC record available at https://lccn.loc.gov/2019025611

Smile, Breathe, and Go Slowly

Slumby the Sloth Goes to School

By CHIARA CARMINATI

Illustrated by ROBERTA ANGARAMO

HOLIDAY HOUSE • NEW YORK

This is Slumby.

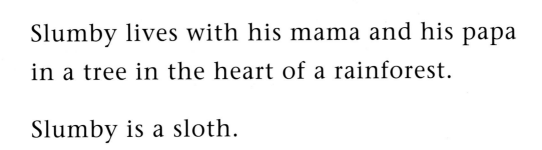

Slumby lives with his mama and his papa
in a tree in the heart of a rainforest.

Slumby is a sloth.

For the most part, sloths are rather sluggish. They sleep a lot and always do their best to avoid any kind of exertion.

Consequently, sloths do everything slowly . . . very . . . very . . . slowly.

The trouble began when Slumby started school.
Slumby had to wake up early and do everything
in a hurry.

He had to wash in a hurry . . . dress in a hurry . . .

and even eat in a hurry!

"Come!" said Mama. "You're already late!"

Slowly . . . very . . . very . . . slowly, Slumby climbed down his tree and began to walk to school.

Slumby stopped only a couple of times . . .
to admire a butterfly . . .
and to observe an unusual insect.

When Slumby finally arrived, he was late . . .
very . . . very . . . late.

"Even today," mumbled Mr. Anteater. But no one
could look at Slumby's serene smile and be angry
for long. Not even Mr. Anteater.

All of Slumby's classmates loved him.
But at recess . . .

Slumby was too slow to play armadillo ball.

Slumby was too slow to jump rope . . .

and was even too slow for the turtle race.

The next day, while Slumby's classmates played ball, jumped rope, and raced, Slumby sat under a tree and watched the butterflies.

Slumby did the same on the next day, the next day, and the next. Slumby wasn't angry, but in time, he became sad.

One day, Slumby was resting in a tree while his classmates played armadillo ball down below. They seemed to be having so much fun until . . .

. . . Possum threw too hard, and Armadillo plunged into the river where a hungry crocodile lay in wait.

"Help!" cried Armadillo.
"Help!" cried the others.

No one had the courage
to rescue poor Armadillo.
No one except for Slumby!

"Don't do it!" shouted his friends. "Turn back! You're much too slow!" Slumby ignored them and jumped.

Because sloths, who are always so slow on land, can be not so slow in the water.

Slumby was an excellent swimmer. He reached his friend in a flash and carried him back to safety.

The crocodile remained with his mouth wide open.

"Hooray for Slumby!" shouted the others, smothering him with kisses. Beneath his soaked and shaggy hair, Slumby blushed with joy.

From that day on, there was always someone to challenge Slumby to a swimming race at recess.

And every once in a while, Slumby's classmates would lie on the grass alongside him, be still, and watch the butterflies. Because every once in a while, it's nice to live life slowly . . .

. . . very . . . very . . . slowly.